I AM
THAT I AM

A JOURNEY THROUGH ADD-OL-LESS-SENSE

A Collection Of Inspired Writings

Ellia English

PRESS

I Am That I Am
A Journey Through Add-Ol-Less-Sense
by Ellia English

Printed in the United States of America

ISBN 978-1-60791-333-7

El Shaddai Entertainment, Inc.
4804 Laurel Canyon Blvd.
Suite 559
Valley Village, CA 91607

www.xulonpress.com

DEDICATION AND ACKNOWLEDGEMENTS

This book is lovingly dedicated to the youth of all ages! Along with Godly diversion and amusement, may you find the encouragement, as well as strength to break free from the bondage of any drab caterpillar like cocoon, and confidently emerge into the colorful '**Butterfly**' of your "**Purpose**".

I give Thanks, praise and honor to my Master for His love, grace, mercy and favor that surround me like a shield. And to the Anointed One, for paying the exurbanite price for my debt, with the ultimate sacrifice, His life, which is in the blood. For without blood there is no remission of sin. Thank you for the blood! Because of it, I am saved by grace through faith!

PREFACE

As I perused many of my personal journals I have poured my heart into over the past years, I began to learn a lot about myself (my true nature). And, I began to get a clearer look at my footprints in this life. I also developed an appreciation for those journals and for having them to glance back upon, because in them I found words of encouragement, which gives me strength and confidence to continue to press forward even today.

When a burning desire arose within me to reach out and help someone else with my writings, I wasn't so confident I should or could do it. But the thought that I might actually be able to encourage somebody, by sharing my writings, helped to energize me with the confidence I needed.

So, I have put together some of my journal writings as a collection, in the hopes that you too may be encouraged.

Hear me and hear me well, I do not claim to know all the answers and I do not profess to be perfect. Believe me, I am still very much a work in progress. And, *"if it had not been for the Lord who was on my side,"* I honestly don't know where I would be today. Yet, I do know that sometimes with a little encouragement and a glimpse into the struggles of others, we are able to learn from someone else' experiences and often just that information alone, can help us to avoid making many of those same mistakes.

One thing I have learned thus far in my journey is that although in this natural human state I am not perfect, yet I am perfect in God's perfection. And what I do **know** is that we all could use a few words of encouragement every now and then.

I received the best words of encouragement ever when my father, the late Reverend Calvin English, said to me, **"Know Jesus For Yourself."** What I learned from my dads' encouraging words is this, it's not about **religion**, it's about **relationship**. It's not about a **man**, it's about **"The Anointing."** From that day forward my desire was to get to know God and to develop my very own personal relationship with God. Believe you me whether you choose to serve God or not, we all are serving something. So here is the question, "What or Whom are you serving?" Here is our mission: "Choose ye this day whom ye shall serve!" The answer, "Is your choice!"

CHAPTER ONE
"ADD"

CHAPTER TWO
"OL'"

CHAPTER FIVE
"TURN AROUND"

CHAPTER ONE

"ADD"

baby   how an afro was born

                     a star with no name

      fight the fat

                                            my rainbow

                              don't forget

                what to do (question)

what to do (answer)

                    i'm your child

                                 a little slow hurry

           nowhere

too know?

                   after the fall

          memphis

                     let me be myself

my song

BABY
(In The Beginning)

The newborn was only a few days old, when mother
cried out indeed! *"Oh Lord what happened to my baby?*
Please tell me where can she be!" Mother searched
the house frantically, praying the baby she would find!
Cause father would be coming home from work any
time!

Oops! Standing so near the furnace, sadly her gown
now she has scorched! But suddenly, mother heard a
still small voice whisper, *"look outside!"* And there she
found her baby, sitting on the porch.

How the baby got there? To mother it is still a mystery!
But that day mother knew this baby of hers was peculiar! And a higher calling upon her life was clear to see!

Being followers of the Word, mother and father had
to admit! *We must "train up our child in the way she*
should go and when she is old she will not depart
from it!"

NOTES:

HOW AN AFRO WAS BORN
(Naturally)

Hey little brown girl, I like that way you're wearing
your hair! Those pretty ribbons and bows adorn your
plaits and braids with care! It looks all nice and shiny
from royal crown or is that palm ade? But when you go
out to play, you'll have to run for the shade! Cause when
the sun gets too hot, you can fry an egg on your scalp!
Sometimes your hair is braided so tight the only relief is
to take a nap.

Yes, some may laugh and tease you. Others may even
point and stare! But little brown girl, never let anyone
make you fill bad about your natural hair! And don't you
ever fill sad about of your mama's southern ways! Cause
here's the story, when you grow older, on your head will
be found a beautiful crown of "tight curled" glory! That
will receive a lot of praise!

NOTES:

A STAR WITH NO NAME
(Catch A Dream)

A star with no name needs a claim to fame. Recognition
to help him be known. Worldwide exposure of his work
could not hurt! Might be exciting to be thrown such a
bone!
Then could come offers for any Broadway show! And
finally he'd be making some dough. A starving artist
he'd be no more! He could even shop in a 5th Avenue
store!

But what if he's a poet, and they don't know it? Or a
writer with lots of books still unread! Could a revela-
tion of his work make him such a big hit, that his name
would be spinning around in their heads?

He could be a singer with a voice of gold,
or a dancer whose steps never grow old! Imagine some
'front page' publicity! Would that be a crime? How
about some rave reviews that would cause him to shine!
Then his name could be in lights all of the time!

A star with no name just needs a claim to fame.

NOTES:

FIGHT THE FAT
(My Determination)

Fight the fat! Can you handle that? Fight to release the thin girl in me! Working for the day she will be free!

It's a long hard struggle. But I'm hanging in there! Soon this fat will turn into thin air! I gotta hang on just a little while longer! I can see my body's definitely getting stronger! But I won't try to make this all happen fast or snappy! Then when I win, I'll be healthy and happy!

Fight the fat! Can you handle that? Fight to release the thin girl in me! Working for the day she will be free!

Everywhere I look, there's lots of food in sight! And that's not helping me to win this fat fight! But if I have to fight for the rest of my life! I'll keep reaching for the power! Each and every hour! To walk a straight and narrow path! And make the diet last!

Fight the fat! Can you handle that? Fight to release the thin girl in me! Working for the day she will be free!

NOTES:

MY RAINBOW
(Colors of Truth)

One day, as I glanced high, I spied an airplane flying
by. Then I saw the most beautiful rainbow, arched high
up in the sky. It reminded me of the goodness of God.
Of His Love and His tender mercies! How happy I am!
I'm reconciled to my Father who loves me faithfully!
And the hope of glory, Christ my savior! Dwells inside
of me! Then I thought, "The promise of the rainbow
still remains the same!" "Nevermore shall this world be
destroyed by rain!" Yet thinking of the Ultimate Promise
set my spirit and soul aflame! "Christ (the anointed one)
is coming back again!"

NOTES:

DON'T FORGET
(Leaning On Mothers' Prayer)

There are times when I am happy, there are times when I feel sad. There are times I feel immortal. But death is a reality, I must add.

There are times and times and time again, I feel like no one cares. Yet, I'm grateful to know there is a God! And I'm glad He answers prayers!

Always at night before I sleep, I pray to the Lord my soul to keep! I'm filled with joy when I see each new day! When I recall lessons learned from my youth, to obey, most memorable are Mother's words, "CHILD DON'T FORGET TO PRAY!"

NOTES:

WHAT TO DO?
(The Question)

What do you do when given the impression that God is through with you? When you call out to Him, you worship Him, you praise Him; yet it seems He wants nothing to do with you. What do you do?

When you pray at night for answers and at daylight you still don't know, what do you do?
When it hurts to have dreams and it appears that none of them may ever come true. When you start to feel worthless and whatever strength you had begins to die too. What do you do?

When you love God so much, you fast and you pray to hear His voice! Yet, it seems He's so far away! What do you do?

Where do you go? How do you stop the pain? If you still had a little faith for tomorrow, would it all be in vain? Will your life have no meaning? Will this all have been a dream? When you wake up, who will you be? What will you have? What will it mean?

Cause if God doesn't want me, there is no need for anything. For without God, I am nothing and I can do no thing. And without faith it's impossible to please God too!

What do you do, when given the impression that God is through with you?

NOTES:

WHAT TO DO?
(The Answer)

You keep on Praying! You keep on Praising! You keep
on Surrendering! You keep on Dreaming! You keep on
Hoping! You keep on Believing! You keep studying the
Word, because the Word is true!

You keep the faith! You keep God's Ways! You keep
your heart with all diligence! Exactly like the Word
says! You keep His promises locked deep in your heart!
For out of your heart is where your life starts!

You keep on Worshipping in Spirit and in Truth! You
keep on Fasting! You keep on Seeking! You keep on
Knocking! You keep on Asking!

Suddenly, you'll encounter an assurance on which
your Heart, Soul and Spirit will agree. HE NEVER
SLEEPS! HE NEVER SLUMBERS! HE'LL NEVER
LEAVE YOU! HE'LL NEVER FORSAKE YOU! Be
encouraged my friend! His word is tried and true! **GOD
"NEVER" gives up on you!**

NOTES:

I'M YOUR CHILD
(An Earnest Prayer)

Our FATHER, her I stand your humble child in need of
prayer. Please give me the strength to go on! Although
I feel like I'm going nowhere. Oh LORD, please stretch
out YOUR loving arms of protection all around me. And
give me the patience I need, to be all that YOU want me
to be!

I'm your child LORD please don't leave me here this
way. I'm your child LORD please don't let me go astray.

Our FATHER, Give me the courage I'll need to go from
day to day. Cause I know I'll find others who are not
living in YOUR righteous way! Please teach me how to
edify them with YOUR word, regarding being prayerful!
So they too will know, *"YOU are our refuge and
strength and a very present help in* (times of) *trouble"*!

I'm your child LORD please don't leave me here this
way. I'm your child LORD please don't let me go astray.

<u>NOTES</u>:

A LITTLE SLOW HURRY
(On A Mission)

If you wanna sit around and gossip, spreading your opinion about the latest dirt or dish! Or brag to strangers about the way your lover socks you with a kiss. If you just got to stick your nose into everybody else's business, don't bother me with this mess!
I'm in a little slow hurry!

I'm in a little slow hurry hun' ain't got no time to stick around. I'm in a little slow hurry hun' I can't let you drag me down. I'm in a little slow hurry hun' on my word you can trust. I'm in a little slow hurry hun' watch my tracks and eat my dust! Aah yes! I'm in a little slow hurry!

If you don't wanna be the best you, that you can be! Or make good choices and accept your responsibilities! If you wanna be shiftless! Lazy! And live in lack and poverty! You go on and do that! But I can't let you hinder me! Get out my way! I'm in a little slow hurry!

I'm in a little slow hurry hun' ain't got no time to stick around. I'm in a little slow hurry hun' I can't let you drag me down. I'm in a little so hurry hun' I'm relying on a promise and a guarantee. I'm in a little slow hurry hun' cause this race is filled with opportunities for me!
Aah yes! I'm in a little slow hurry!

NOTES:

NOWHERE
(No Thing!)

Excuse me while I live! Depression is not for me! Once
you've searched your own soul I hope you will agree.
You've got to take life one day at a time! Keep it simple
allow yourself to live! Don't always be a selfish taker,
open your heart and give!

Freedom is indeed a choice! So everyone, come on!
Raise your voice! And scream, "you choose to be free!"
Don't let misunderstandings cloud your path, and lead
you captive in total despair! That leads to nowhere!

NOTES:

TOO KNOW?
(A Absolute Question)

If we could see the future and know the out come of all our plans, would it change the desires of our hearts? Too know when life becomes death or when death becomes life, as in nature, when it makes a fresh new start?

What would we give knowing what we'd receive? How could we live with no need to believe?

Sometimes, it's not always good to know what's going to happen in your life. It will certainly leave no room to make a wish or have a surprise.

So let's say, you know everything that's going to happen on every tomorrow! Tell me, how could you ever appreciate (in awesome wonder), God's marvelous Sunrise?

NOTES:

AFTER THE FALL
(Fresh and New)

IT'S ABOUT STARTING ALL OVER AGAIN!

I want the Lord to take me and use me as I am!

I know that I'm not perfect. I'm only striving for perfection. As long as the Lord is my guide, I know I'll always have protection!

He hears me when I call. He picks me up whenever I fall. I love the Lord God Almighty! He's my strength! My all and all!

That's why I'll serve him each and everyday of my life, no matter what the cost! As long as I keep my trust in Him, I know I'll never be lost!

NOTES:

MEMPHIS
(With Love! My God Daughter)

There was a little girl with pretty brown eyes, and the most
beautiful smile that you ever did see. One day her mom was
on the phone attempting to have a conversation with me.
When I heard, Memphis Know! Memphis Know! Know
Memphis! Memphis Know!

There was a little girl with beautiful hair, the most beautiful
hair that you ever did see. She was playing with her Dad
they were singing a song, when she started pushing buttons
on the family TV. He said, Memphis Know! Memphis
Know! Know Memphis! Memphis Know! And when her
mom heard what was going on she came in and starting
yelling along, they said, Memphis Know! Memphis Know!
Know Memphis! Memphis Know!

I had a dream about this pretty little girl she was all grown
up, had earned a PHD. She was saving lives, receiving
awards! And we were all proud as any parent could be.
We yelled, Memphis Go! Memphis Go! Go Memphis!
Memphis Go!

NOTES:

LET ME BE MYSELF
(Genuine/Authentic)

You keep trying to form me into what you want me to be. You try to label me and box me into your idea of me. You didn't make me! You didn't create me! So let me be myself!

Let me be myself When I'm me I'm free.

Let me be myself Get to know the real me.

Let me be myself I know exactly who I am.

So, let me be myself.

Quit tryin' to place your inhibitions on me! Quit tryin' to force your plans on my life "Respect me!" My purpose is divine! And has been divinely planned! I'm made in the **image of God!** I am **more than** an **ordinary** woman! So, let me be myself!

Let me be myself When I'm me I'm free.

Let me be myself Get to know the real me.

Let me be myself I know exactly who I am.

So, let me be myself.

NOTES:

MY SONG
(Amazing)

So amazing is the song I hear in my heart,

when my mind is clear and my creativity runs free!

It lifts me higher than the moon and the stars.

It dries my tears and deletes my scars!

It removes my doubts and destroys my fears,

it replaces my depression with joy and glee!

Yes, so amazing is the song I hear in my heart!

My song is entitled: "<u>I LOVE ME</u>"!

NOTES:

CHAPTER TWO

"OL'"

too lady like

from: you, to: you

the bottle

sex drugs and rock n roll

ode to life

i've gotta take control

there is a light

TOO LADY LIKE
(Speak Life)

You want to say (oh dram)! But instead you say
oh darn!

You want to say (oh blit)! But instead you say oh
shucks!

You want to say (oh pluck)! But instead you say
oh fart!

You want to say (mudda plucker)! But to say it may
tear them apart.

So you stand there thinking of all the various cuss
words you could say,

and how easily those cuss words would blow them
(sons of she dogs) away!

In spite of that, you stand tall! You hold your peace!
And bite hard into your tongue!

Knowing, (dam the well) it will never be said you
cursed and caused somebody harm!

NOTES:

FROM: YOU TO: YOU
(Mirror Mirror)

You say it's me you don't want to hurt. But isn't it really
you? Don't you know that by living in denial, you can
never hear the truth? You keep hiding behind the same
lying excuse! When will you learn? That's a form of self
abuse!

Stop stretching the truth! Be real to your self. If you
can't be honest with you, don't expect anybody else to!
Stop stretching the truth!

You lie about the way you feel! Trying to act like it
doesn't matter! You pretend you got it all together!
When your emotions are torn and tattered! Well you can
fool some of the people, some of the time. But you can't
fool me! So don't waste my time!

Stop stretching the truth! Be real to your self. If you
can't be honest with you, don't expect anybody else to!
Stop stretching the truth!

One dumb excuse! *"Oh it's just a little white lie!"* After
the other! *"Well it's only a half truth!"* Open your eyes!
You know good and well you're not blind! Can't you see
all the harm, your lies do!

Stop stretching the truth! Be real to your self If you can't
be honest with you don't expect anybody else to! Stop
stretching the truth.

NOTES:

THE BOTTLE
(Glimmer of Hope)

I opened up a bottle that was once squeezed tightly shut.
And many people said of me, *"Look at her! There goes
the nut"*. But I care nothing of what they say! Cause
I learned early in my youth! Inside this very bottle is
where I'll find the truth!

I'll find all the things this world has done! And all the
things this world is going to do! But none of this will be
a surprise to me! Because nothing in this world is new!

That's why I like this bottle, and I'll take it wherever
I go. Because I've learned, that the more I give to this
bottle, the more this bottle will help me grow!

NOTES:

SEX, DRUGS & ROCK N ROLL
(Absence Of Balance)

I heard some people sayin,' *"We just won't be nice no more!"* When the truth of the matter is, they've never been nice before. Better get real! I'm telling you like it is! It's time to unclog your ears! Cause soon you're gonna realize, you've wasted many years!

Wake up! Smell the coffee! Life keeps rolling along! In next to no time you're gonna find, above your head a huge gravestone. That reads: *"Here lies the idiot who wouldn't live right. Partying with lots of drugs, sex, rock n roll! Out Of Control! All day and all through the night!"*

NOTES:

ODE TO LIFE
(A Word Of Wisdom)

She was beautiful, talented and gifted. Destined to become a bright shinning Star. But the booze, the drugs and the fast life didn't allow her to get very far.

One day she got hold of a bad drug that chemically altered her brain. And now she sits in a crowded psyche ward having been declared mentally insane.

Dead to the world! In a Shroud of Darkness! Darker than the Darkest Night! Never becoming the 'Light!...' she always dreamed she'd be! She paid a dear and precious price! Her life!

Because, that joy ride she took was not free!
The moral of my story is as plain and simple as this.
Many will *"With Love"* offer you drugs, booze and the fast life. But that kind of *"Love"*, seals your *Death* with a Kiss!

NOTES:

I'VE GOTTA TAKE CONTROL
(A Crush)

I've got to take control of this lovesick feeling! I've got to take control! I've got to take control! I've got to take control, cause my mind is reeling! I've got to take control! I've got to take control!

My thoughts become muddled! I get weak in the knees! Every time he passes me on the street. My heart skips a beat! I almost lose my balance, it's like I'm walking on two left feet.

I've got to take control of this lovesick feeling! I've got to take control! I've got to take control! I've got to take control, cause my mind is reeling! I've got to take control! I've got to take control!

I can't eat! I can't sleep! Anytime he's near, he sends shivers up and down my spine! It's like vertigo! Or an infected inner ear! I can't hold my head up, cause it's spinning all the time.

I've got to take control of this lovesick feeling! I've got to take control! I've got to take control! I've got to take control, cause my mind is reeling! I've got to take control! I've got to take control!

NOTES:

THERE IS A LIGHT
(Get Understanding)

There is a light that's bold and bright! It leads the way
for the lost and the stray!

But you must search deep within your heart to see. Or
spend your life in obscurity for all eternity!

Don't fret the answer's here! And so much closer than
you think! Closer than the twinkle of an eye, or a blink.
*("The **Word** is nigh thee, even in thy mouth and in thy
heart")*

Let it sift through that chaos of confusion, rejecting
salvation in your soul! Don't wait until you're too frail
or feeble or ineffectually old!

In searching you will definitely find clear perception at
last! For The ***Word***, is a Lamp unto your feet and a Light
unto your path!

NOTES:

CHAPTER THREE

"LESS"

```
                                        waiting
        the time is ripe
                        i did it
                        crazy over you
                                            pleasure
                don't take me through these changes
        mr. travelin' man
                        lil' mama
            not the answer
                                    mean't to be friends
                                            love lament
        you're gone
                        peace of mind
            welcome
                                    no
```

WAITING
(First Love)

He was very kind, when he spoke my name. Said, he
was '*for real*', and would not play games. He brought to
me a gift, he had wrapped in red. *"I want to make you
happy,"* is what he said. Before he went away.

Feeling so demure, when he took my hand! I said, *"I
need some time!"* He said, *"I understand."* Then he
looked into my eyes, and said, *"You can rest assured,
this love I have for you is sincere and pure!"* Before he
went away.

Now, I'm waiting for him to come back again. The
young man with the key to set my heart free. I'm
waiting! I know he will return someday. The love we
share will never go away.

The romance we shared was so special and new. And
although our time was short, in my heart I knew, that he
was the one for me and I would say, *"I do!"* Before he
went away.

Like a dream come true, he came into my life. Proposing
from his heart to me, *"Please be my wife!"* On that
enchanting day I was dressed all in white! My life
became anew on our wedding night! Before he went
away.

*When we are together skies are clear and blue! My life
has novel meaning! Yes it's spanking new! Our love
is like a treasure, buried at sea! To my heart he is the
only love to hold the key!*

He looked so debonair in his uniform. We said our last goodbye on the train platform. I prayed that he'd be safe, and kept free from harm. Before he went away.

Now, I'm waiting for him to come back again. The young man with the key, to set my heart free. I'm waiting! I know he will return someday. The love we share will never go away.

THE TIME IS RIPE
(Just Plain Hot)

Woke up in the middle of the night. I was thinking of you. Broke into a cold sweat! Strange anxieties!

Mind racing! Body aching! Powerful emotions! Fire of desire inside me demands to break free! Been holding back this feeling far too long! The desire to burst through is much too strong!

The time is ripe for me to love you tonight. The time is ripe! Gotta face reality! The time is ripe for me to love you tonight. The time is ripe! Boy I want you to be with me.

Letting go of all apprehensions! Putting my mind at ease! No need for fear! Just altered priorities!

Guess now I'm ready, for an affair that's sensual and great! A body that just can't wait is primed to celebrate! Hope my time with you will be real nice! Expect this venture to lead me to paradise!

The time is ripe for me to love you tonight. The time is ripe! Gotta face reality!
The time is ripe for me to love you tonight. The time is ripe! Boy I want you to be with me.

NOTES:

I DID IT
(And I'll Do It Again?)

When Auntie told mommy that I kissed a soldier, I thought
that my life was over! I found it was best that I just
confess! All about my clandestine lover!

Yeah I did it, I did it, and I'll do it again! I did it, I did it
and I'll do it again!

I was standing on a corner, watching all the boys go by.
This fellow came up to me and asked me how I spend my
nights. He pulled me real close to him and he kissed me in
the face! When my Auntie saw this, I guess her mind was
blown into space!

Yeah I did it, I did it and I'll do it again! I did it, I did it
and I'll do it again!

It was only Tommy Taylor! I've known him ever since first
grade! Now he's become a soldier! Marching in his own
parade! He told me that he loved me! He wanted me to be his
bride! I fell into his arms! I thought my heart would burst with
pride!

Yeah I did it, I did it and I'll do it again! I did it I did it and
I'll do it again!

He nearly made me scream! Called me his homecoming
queen! He was the boy next door! The one I always did
adore! He was my very best friend! And we vowed our
love would never end!

Yeah I did it, I did it and I'll do it again! I did it I did it and
I'll do it again!

NOTES:

CRAZY OVER YOU
(Wild and Zany)

Baby you, oh you, came into my life you made me feel
brand new. You added that extra spice! You filled me
with desire and that feeling takes me higher!

I'm going crazy over you and all the things you do, baby
you've given me a brand new style. I'm going crazy
over you and all the things you do baby you've given me
a brand new smile!

You changed my way of thinking, when it comes to
lovin' you. And I start to doing all the things a woman's
suppose to do. You thrill me with your lovin and I get
plenty of it. Baby you really set my soul on fire!

I'm going crazy over you and all the things you do, baby
you've given me a brand new style, I'm going crazy
over you and all the things you do baby you've given me
a brand new smile!

NOTES:

PLEASURE
(It's Fleeting)

You can get a lasting heartache for a few moments of pleasure. So you'd better think, it's reality! Ain't that a shame! How long the pain will last is time you can't measure. Then you feel you've lost your soul! Tell me what have you gained?

No matter how tempting any situation might be, (common sense says), take off those rose colored glasses, so you can clearly see! When they tell you the grass is always greener on the other side! Know that it's only a smoke screen for the skeletons they're trying to hide. But child, you'd better bury that bold faced **lie** in a great big hole. Cause the truth be told, everything that glitters is not absolutely gold.

You can get a lasting heartache for a few moments of pleasure. So you'd better think, it's reality! Ain't that a shame! How long the pain will last is time you can't measure. Then you feel you've lost your soul! Tell me what have you gained?

Listen to the wisdom that lies deep inside of you! Don't be misled by deceptive points of view! Resist the darkness and strive diligently for the light! Or you'll find right choices only in hindsight.

Cause you can get a lasting heartache for a few moments of pleasure, pleasure, pleasure, pleasure...

NOTES:

DON'T TAKE ME THROUGH THESE CHANGES
(No Commitment, No Respect)

Don't take me through these changes it's quite so unfair.
Don't take me through these changes I wonder if you
ever cared.

My self esteem is completely shattered! My mind,
you've whipped and horribly battered! Still, I don't want
to lose you! Who'd want me in this used condition?
Please don't continue to add to my pain! Your insolence
is driving me insane! And I'm not sure I can live through
this situation!

Don't take me through these changes it's quite so unfair.
Don't take me through these changes I wonder if you
ever cared.

You told me you really loved me! I wanted so much to
believe! Then you said if I loved you, I would satisfy
your needs! When I told you, *"I was a virgin!"* *"It's
not important!"* was your reply. As you stood glaring
with that sinister look in your eyes. I was afraid you
wouldn't love me! So I did just as you pleased. Now
you're treating me like I'm a stranger, with an incurable
disease! Tell me what did I do wrong? How long will
you keep hurting me, how long?

Don't take me through these changes it's quite so
unfair. Don't take me through these changes I wonder
if you ever cared.

You don't understand, can't you see I have feelings
man! And when you mistreat me it really, really hurts!
Why do you abuse me and walk on me like I'm a piece
of dirt? I'm not made of stone or clay! I'm human, so
please treat me that way.

Don't take me through these changes it's quite so unfair.
Don't take me through these changes I wonder if you
ever cared.

MR. TRAVELIN' MAN
(Step)

Something tells me I'm not your final destination. You
plan to use me solely as a rest station.

Oh but listen boy, I'm not a wind up toy, that you can
lead around on a string! And I'm not a parking garage,
for your long black limousine!

Mr. Travelin' man, I do not plan to be your part time
convenient store! Hear my advice. You better think
twice! Before you come around knocking at my door.

Don't think that you can stop by here anytime you
want... To pimp me like I'm some kind of whore!

NOTES:

LIL' MAMA
(Come On, Get Up!)

Whatcha gon' do lil' mama? How ya' gon' fix yo' hair?
Whatcha gon' do lil' mama? What kinda clothes will ya'
wear? Whatcha gon' do lil' mama? It's time to get outta
yo' bed! Whatcha gon' do lil' mama? Thoughts runnin'
round in yo' head?

You better get up! Get out! And learn what's new! You
better get up! Get out! There is so much you can do! You
better get up! Get out this morning! It's well after eight!
You better get up! Get out! Before it's too late!

Why you wastin' time? What's that on yo' mind? Why
don't you get up little girl? And see what's goin' on in
this great big world!

Whatcha gon' do lil' mama? When somebody ring yo'
phone? Whatcha gon' do lil' mama? Listen to the answer
machine say, *"you not home!"*

Come on get up! Get dressed! And start makin' hay!
Who knows! This could be a wonderful day!

<u>NOTES:</u>

NOT THE ANSWER
(Bust It)

Who do you think you're foolin', playin' those nasty
games. Seems you find it funny, takin' my love in vain.
The way you treat women, it's finally clear to me, that
you suffer from an acute case of misogyny.

Boy, you are not the answer! It's not about all that! You
think! You're cracked up to be!

You're on a major power trip, your ego' about to
explode! Better be careful of a blow out, baby, you're
kickin' into over load. Your wolf ticket manner makes
you fill big like you're some kind of Boss! Better climb
down off your high horse, baby! I'm not the one to
cross.

Boy, you are not the answer! It's not about all that! You
think! You're cracked up to be!

Can you weather a storm? Can you keep me from harm?
And If I asked you to, could you lead me in the right
way? Hell No! You can only lead me astray! So pick
up your B.S. and get the F. out of my face. Someone
stronger and better is takin' your place!

Boy, you are not the answer! It's not about all that! You
think! You're cracked up to be!

<u>NOTES:</u>

MEANT TO BE FRIENDS
(Oh To Be Equally Yoked!*)*

Just because it seems we're not meant to be married
doesn't have to mean we're not meant to be friends.

There are so many wonderful moments we shared you
and I. Laughter was our music sweet duets that made us
cry. But as time passed on and ever much too soon! We
both started to sing different tunes.

Just because it seems we're not meant to be married
doesn't have to mean we're not meant to be friends.

I will never forget the magic, love created in our
lives. Or that very special day we vowed to be
husband and wife. There is a lesson in this, and it's
something we all should know. A union not meant to
be, surely can never grow!

Just because it seems we're not meant to be married
doesn't have to mean we're not meant to be friends.

A love so strong should last forever! What went wrong?
The harmony! We tried to force it? What a cacophony!
An unfortunate course! Now we're in the middle of a
painful divorce!

Just because it seems we're not meant to be married
doesn't have to mean we're not meant to be friends.

I see it takes **more than love** for a lasting, 'tour de
force,' Marriage Communion. It's also necessary to be
Equally Yoked in a Balanced Union!

83

Just because it seems we're not meant to be married
doesn't have to mean we're not meant to be friends.

LOVE LAMENT
(Bona Fide Agony)

Sometimes I wish I had no feelings at all, then maybe
I wouldn't fall in love. Or end up hurt, because I don't
understand what love means. But I do know this, love is
painful and love is confusing.

I've cried so many tears because of how love makes
me feel. When love over powers me, it takes complete
control of my emotions. It ties me up in knots, which
seems impossible for me to break free.

But what if I could take these feelings and lock them in
a safe. And throw it with an anchor into the darkest and
deepest sea! Then I'd never have to worry about falling
in love, or being hurt because a love is wrong for me.

Yes, Love is painful! It's so confusing! I'm not sure
which way to go. I don't know if he'll ever love me, so I
try not to let it show.

NOTES:

YOU'RE GONE
(Letting Go)

You're gone! Yes you're gone! I know you always
wanted to leave. It was your choice I heard it in your
voice! I only gave you your wish. Sorry no regrets.
Let go of that fretful nature. It doesn't become you.
You' re gone!

My love was true, as I faithfully gave it all to you.
But you tossed it all aside, cause your pertinacious
pride wouldn't let me in. So my friend, I let you win.
You're gone.

At first I didn't think that I could go on without you.
But as time passed by I began to try. Everyday I grew
stronger. Now I know I can and I will make it through.
Even though you're gone.

If I had known all of the heartache being with you would
bring me, I never would have given all my love so
freely. Or waited so long for that special day, for you to
come to me and say you'd love me forever! If only I'd
known. Now you're gone! Yes, you're gone!

NOTES:

WELCOME
(Equilibrium)

Hello sunshine! Hello rain! You are both welcome to come back again. It's been way too long to have a life filled with pain. If it weren't for you I'd go insane. A joyless life should be deemed a crime. Welcome rain! Welcome sunshine! You brought joy back into this life of mine.

Lying on the beach and the sun was shining bright we'd been together a week and we still had another night. When the sun went down I went inside, and it began to rain, but oh it wasn't in vain. Cause I loved them both the same.

Then the sun came out again and I went outside for a while, I felt the sun on my face and all I could do was smile. But then all of a sudden I felt a drop of rain, and I thought the day would be a disaster! But oh it wasn't in vain! For the rain washed away tears crowding my face, that had no name.

Hello sunshine! Hello rain! You are both welcome to come back again. It's been way too long to have a life filled with pain. If it weren't for you I'd go insane. A joyless life should be deemed a crime. Welcome rain! Welcome sunshine! You brought joy back into this life of mine.

NOTES:

NO
(No!)

Just because I choose to shake it, don't mean you have
the right to take it! When I say no, I mean no! It's not for
you to object. Why don't you be a real man and show
me some respect! When I say no, I mean NO!

When we left the party that night going for a spin, I
never thought to worry cause you were my best friend.
We put all the windows down to inhale the crisp night
air. I was having so much fun, enjoying the music and
the wind in my hair.

That's why I was so surprised and did not understand.
Especially when you placed your hands where they
should never be. And when I said *"NO!"* You wouldn't
let go! You said, *"girl stop teasing me!"*

Just because I choose to shake it, don't mean you have
the right to take it! When I say no, I mean no! It's not for
you to object. Why don't you be a real man and show
me some respect! When I say no, I mean NO!

NOTES:

PEACE OF MIND
(Heart, Love Song)

My life seemed empty. Felt uneasy day and night. A persistent battle grew deep within. I felt no comfort was in sight. I had a broken heart, shattered dreams, my mind whirling in a wild spin. I never thought that I'd find rest! Never thought I'd love again. Then you came along, gave my heart a brand new song! Now I got a new peace of mind in this love I found.

I found happiness it's true. A type of joy I never knew! I got a new peace of mind in this love I found.

Now that my heart is singing, my dreams are endless too. Divine visions of our love plays like a rhapsody for two. Don't know what the future holds or what tomorrow has in store! But I'll let tomorrow take care of itself cause this is the love I've been waiting for!

I found happiness it's true. A type of joy I never knew! I got a new peace of mind in this love I found.

A peace of mind can be a hard thing to find when love seems untrue. But when you've found the perfect love like mine, old things pass away and all things become brand new!

I found happiness it's true. A type of joy I never knew! I got a new peace of mind in this love I found.

CHAPTER FOUR

"SENSE"

no rhyme or reason

three in one

keep cooking

real love

water + bread + light + word

go

no way

listen to your heart

who holds the key

never you mind

the crooked manager

misery loves company?

so not good for me

the word is a rock

live strong and prosper

more

you know you

those lost days

don't drop the ball

NO RHYME OR REASON
(It Just Don't Make No Sense)

There is no rhyme or reason for these things I give
thought to. They are just some things I find that makes
absolutely no since to me.
Like why the plural for house is houses and the plural
for mouse is mice. Or why we pronounce (K A N S A
S) CAN/SIS, and we pronounce (A R K A N S A S)
ARE/CAN/SAW.

This language of ours can be very confusing especially
now that everyone speaks it as he pleases. Is English no
longer the language of America and all are free to speak
"Anything eses?" (ie: meaning, whatever you like.)

There is no rhyme or reason for these things I give
thought to. They are just some things I find that makes
absolutely no since to me.

NOTES:

THREE IN ONE
(3 Divergent Free Verses)

(I)
DISCOMBULATING

There is a message that we all should know, because you'll find that everywhere you go people will began to wander where you're coming from. Although, you may feel that you're fine! Others will accuse you of a crime you could not possibly commit.

(II)
CHOOSE YE THIS DAY

People killing each other, stealing from their brothers! Abusing their mothers! But never punished and never sued. Yet some have been falsely accused while others are being mentally abused.

Is life to be that way? God gives us a choice. Is life to be that way? Saints raise your voice!
Let's stop all the evil that is spreading across the land. And let's stop giving in to the wrong doings of man. For God so loved this world, he sent his only son to die, so the right to life would be given to you and I.

Is life to be that way? God gives us a choice. Is life to be that way? Saints raise your voice!

(III)
MISSING?

Which one is missing? **Me, Myself** or **I**? It hurts **Me** to be missing! I cannot tell a lie! **Myself** looks at **Me** everyday! Wondering if **I** up and went away! But **Me** misses the lovely smile of **Myself,** and that makes **Me** feel gray. And **I** miss the joy shared when it's time to pray! **Me, Myself** and **I** often count the days together. **I** has always been there through good and stormy weather! So it seems that **Me** of all people should've watched out for **Myself.** Yet **I** refused to be accused! So **I** just turned and left! It was an inner conflict that signaled the missing alert! The mind was filled with chaos and it had gone berserk! So, when **I** focused and started to listen, **I** received an epiphany! And just as **I** explained it to **Myself. Me, Myself and I** will co exist in harmony!

KEEP COOKING
(Heavens Daughters' Recipe)

First you put your peaches into the pot! Add ten cups
of sugar right on top! Add a little sherry for a taste just
right, then stir it up honey child with all your might!
Step back, stretch your arms and let it simmer a while.
You got it goin' on baby, have a sip of sherry and smile.
Then grab hold of that lid and give it a slam'! And that's
what Ellamay calls 'Canning The Jam.' *"See, it ain't too
hard to make the Jam!"*

Thank you so much for joining "Keep Cooking With
Ellamay!" Don't forget to join us again, be prompt now
don't delay! Cause next week Ellamays' cooking topic
will be: "Hedging the Hog and all it's Innards", ya see!
And, she will show you how to make Chitlins with Polk
Salad and her special Bromiss stew!

So until then, Ellamay says, *"Keep Cooking With Me!
And I'll Keep Cooking With You!"*

NOTES:

REAL LOVE
(The Love For Me)

Another sunny day! I'm so glad I'm here! The birds are
singing and the sky is clear! I feel a strong sensation
being showered from above! It can only be the greatest
gift of all! Which is Love!

I'm talking bout love, love, love!... Real Love!

Love that's patient, love that's kind! Love that's giving
all the time! Love that doesn't hold on to the bad! But
rejoices in truth and turns sad into glad! Love that casts
out doubts and fears! Love that calms and dries all tears!

I'm talking bout love, love, love!... Real Love!

Real Love is the only Love for me! Real Love has set
me free indeed! Real Love fulfills my every need!

I'm talking bout love, love, love!... Real Love!

NOTES:

WATER+BREAD+LIGHT+WORD
(A Love Equation)

Living Water! Living Water! Let me drink til I thirst no more! Living Water! Living Water! Fill my heart til it overflows! Your Word you speak is Spirit and Life to me! The day I received you in my heart, was the day you set me free! Living Water! Vital Water! I now have life eternally.

Bread Of Heaven! Bread Of Heaven! Please feed me til I want no more! Bread of Heaven! Bread of Heaven! You gave your life for this world I know! You died upon a rugged cross! For our sin debt you paid a great cost! Bread of Heaven! Bread of Heaven! You robbed the grave of its' victory! Bread of Heaven! Yahushua Ha Mashiach! Morning by morning new mercies I see!

Light Of The World! Light Of The World! You shine so bright for all to see! You are the Way, the Truth and the Life! And no man cometh to the Father but by Thee! Light of the World! King of Kings! You breathed your last breath on Calvary! And now you are seated at the right hand of the Father, making intersession for me!

Living Word! Living Word! Thank you for becoming the Perfect sacrifice! Living Word! Living Word! I choose to serve you the rest of my life! Continually offering the sacrifice of Praise! The fruit of my lips giving thanks to your name!

Living Word! Lamb of God! Oh taste and see that you are good! Forgiving us our debts as we forgive our debtors! Especially when we don't behave as righteously as we should! Yet we are privileged with a sweet sacrament, in righteous remembrance of you! When we drink Your blood, as our wine! And eat Your body, as our food!

GO
(Forgiveness)

Like the story of the woman caught in adultery, when
"Stone her!" everyone said. But Jesus stooped to the
ground and began to write instead. Then He allowed *"he
who is without sin, among you, let him cast out the first
stone"*, yet when He looked up from His writing, He and
the woman were left all alone.

"Where are your accusers?", Jesus asked. *"The ones
that were here before?"* The woman replied, *"They are
all gone Good Teacher!"* *"Then I too forgive you."* He
said, *"So go in peace and sin no more!"*

It's those secret sins that get us into trouble, the ones we
think no one sees us doing. But often we are reminded
of them when the battle in our minds we are pursuing.

Yet, we too could be released and find peace, if we were
to confess our sins with a repentant heart, and from that
destructive behavior we commit to totally depart.

Then just like the woman, in that story, who'd been
accused by the score. Jesus would say, *"I too forgive
you, so go in peace and sin no more!"*

NOTES:

NO WAY?
(NO WAY!)

Who says it's wrong to dream? Who says I'm asking for
too much? As I review my plans and schemes all I want
is just a touch of simple joy in my life today. And are
you telling me NO WAY?

What makes it wrong with what I do, when I smile and
laugh and giggle? How am I hurting anyone, if in my
sleep my toes I wiggle? It's my love and joy within,
manifesting an outward display! And are you telling
me NO WAY?

In the mornings, I choose to extend a warm greeting
with a smile. What? Am I wrong for brightening up the
day of a child? If I choose to lend a helping hand! Or
lighten the load of my fellowman! If he has had a long
and arduous day! Are you telling me NO WAY?

What laws are you trying to enforce? Whose selfish
doctrine have you endorsed? That you would attempt to
prevent me, from enjoying this life abundantly! Well,
woe unto you! To reject the price paid for your life
would be a stupid sacrifice. Cause that enormous debt
you certainly cannot afford to pay.
What? Oh, are you petitioning me as a new recruit? You
have the audacity to think that I would join you?
To that I say, "Absolutely NO WAY!"

NOTES:

LISTEN TO MY HEART
(The Love Within)

My honesty seems too much, therefore my gifts you will
not touch. I know it's because so often your heart's been
broken with false promises.

Well let me make this perfectly clear, such confusion
you won't find here
Just listen to my heart and you'll understand where I'm
coming from.

And if with your heart you cannot hear, listen to my
heart and have no fear.
Listen to my heart, you will find only true love there.

Listen to my heart, when it's hard for you to feel. Listen
to my heart and to your heart it will reveal. This love I
have for you no one can steal. Just listen to my heart!

Listen to my heart! Listen to my heart!

NOTES:

WHO HOLDS THE KEYS
(The Mystery)

Life is full of great mysteries! So bold and blindingly
bright! If by chance you discover them in the early dawn
or blackest night! You'll find layer upon layer of vast
conundrums to be solved, before you even reach the
actual clue as to how your life becomes involved.

But, before many of us can find out anything we throw
up our hands in sheer frustration! Shouting *"I quit!"*
Rejecting a fruitful life, in a fit of exasperation! Growing
more stagnant and stubborn, until grey hairs or no hair
covers our head! Only waking sometime thereafter to
learn, oops! Guess what? Your dead!

If only you had taken the time to seek the Mystery of
Truth that makes you free! If only you had embraced
the Mystery of Purpose and the Anointed One of
liberty! Well don't worry! It's not too late! If these
words you can read. Prepare the soil of your heart and
plant them as a seed!

Don't miss this living opportunity to seek education on
your knees! It is in persistent prayer, where you'll find
who holds the keys.

NOTES:

NEVER YOU MIND
(Keep Yo Head Up!)

You know that you are a true woman of God. A humble
servant! You strive very hard, trudging through all the
muck and mire! Even a scorching fire, that this life may
display!

So never you mind what the people say!

To be a virtuous woman is not an easy task. Especially,
when dealing with church folk! (ie: *"we wear the
mask")* Just remember you are priced far above rubies,
well beyond the ignorance of the potter's clay.

So never you mind what the people say!

You respect yourself! You don't seek definition! And the
love you share has 'no condition'! It's harvest time! Go
ahead, let your light so shine today!

And never you mind what the people say!

NOTES:

THE CROOKED MANAGER
(Learn It!)

"Help you manage your money?" "Of course I will!"
The manager did reply. *"Just give me all your deeds
and your trusts!"* (He said with a grin), *"On me you can
always rely!"*

*"Give me all your bank accounts! Your salaries! I want
signature approval! Let me handle your investment port-
folio! Why yes, I've got lot's of scruples!" "Trust me!
Give me your passwords and your pen codes. I guarantee I will steadfastly manage them all!"*

Now, that's the trouble with being gullible, for such an
offer, you will fall.

And neglect to notice, with a prudent eye, the manager
stealing and padding his coat! Next thing you know, debt
starts to grow and the manager says, *"you're flat broke!"*

Well, that's my tale of the crooked manager, who doesn't
look crooked when first you meet. But the TRUTH is:
**"Anytime you let someone other than yourself manage
your money, a watchful eye on your money (and the
manager), you must keep!"**

NOTES:

MISERY LOVES COMPANY?
(Ode to Bubbly)

Must you always be so happy, always smiling and filled
with glee? While the rest of us are content to wallow in
gloom and misery!

Either you join us in our quest, to welter in depression
and despair, or take your happy hips, your smile and
your joy, and get the heck out of here.

We don't like your kind around us! You give our misery
a bad name! Besides, your presence makes us feel, for
our misery, we are the only ones to blame!

We don't choose to know that truth! We feel we have
no other choice! So don't come in here with your fain
disposition, singing in your mezzo soprano voice!

Or we will give you something to **not** be happy for,
being so bubbly like champagne! We will try and block
your inspiration and scandalize your name!

So don't mess with us we are misery, and that's what
we want to be! And all we ever yearn for is the **same**
company!

NOTES:

SO NOT GOOD FOR ME
(Ghastly)

The worse thing I could ever see, is wasting this
wonderful life God has gifted me. Not appreciating
the oxygen I'm allowed to breathe, each new day I am
blessed to live and receive!

THAT WOULD BE SO NOT GOOD FOR ME!

Not acknowledging, a gloriously magnificent Sunrise!
Sunset! Moon! Or Star lit night! Or Beautiful flowers,
lofty trees, majestic mountains or birds in flight! Or,
even the dazzling emerald June bug, humming a tune
with ease. Or the rushing mighty waves tossing audibly
upon the seas.

THAT WOULD BE SO NOT GOOD FOR ME!

Not saying Thank you, for a kind gesture, a compliment,
or a smile. Not even realizing the miracle in my ability
to walk a 10k mile! Not seeing God's hand in a new
child being birthed! Not valuing every corner of God's
great green earth!

THAT WOULD BE SO NOT GOOD FOR ME!

Or Living a life with no purpose in mind! Leaving no
mark or footprint for those left behind! Oh what a miser-
able judgment day I would see... and...

THAT WOULD BE **SO NOT GOOD FOR ME.**

NOTES:

THE WORD IS A ROCK
(Word)

Be doers of the Word and not hearers only. Put the Word
into use building a strong foundation, that neither wind
nor rain could prevail against it!

Cause it's built on a rock! The Word is a rock, the rock
of our salvation! Yes, it's built on a rock! A solid rock,
strong enough to carry a nation!

Don't be like the foolish man who built his house upon
the sand, and it all came tumbling down. In the beginning was the Word and the Word was God, obey the
Word and build your house on solid ground.

Cause it's built on a rock! The Word is a rock, the rock
of our salvation! Yes, it's built on a rock! A solid rock,
strong enough to carry a nation!

The Word is a rock, (on this Rock I'll build my church)!
The Word is a rock, (the stone the builders rejected)!
The Word is a rock, (the spiritual rock that gives life)!
The Word is a rock, and that spiritual rock is Christ!

So be doers of the Word and not hearers only. Put the
Word into use building a strong foundation, that neither
wind nor rain could prevail against it!

Cause it's built on a rock! The Word is a rock, the rock
of our salvation! Yes, it's built on a rock! A solid rock,
strong enough to carry a nation!

NOTES:

LIVE STRONG AND PROSPER
(Have Faith, Choose Life)

*"Beloved, I wish above all else that you would prosper
and be in good health, even as your soul prospers"*

Live strong and prosper! It's been given unto you, to do
so, if you just believe.

Live strong and prosper, spreading peace and harmony
for all posterity!

You have a choice each day, of life and death!
You have a choice to prevail, in sickness and health! A
choice of blessings or curses, poverty or wealth!

You have the choice! Heed the voice! Eat and drink
from God's fountain of love! Deny yourself! Take
up your cross! And chase His Good and Perfect Gift
from above!

Live strong and prosper! It's been given unto you, to do
so, if you just believe.

Live strong and prosper, spreading peace and harmony
for all posterity!

NOTES:

MORE
(A Conqueror)

More than Royalty! More than Nobility! More than the Crown a great Monarch would endorse.

More than powerful! More than Invincible! More than Valor to steer a rugged course!

I am Strong, I am Wise, I am the Apple of my Father's eye. I can do all things through the strength He gives me. And each day I aspire to reach higher and higher! A standard of my hearts desire! Becoming all I'm created to be.

More than Dangerous! More than Perilous! More than inflicting injury! To expose a risky source!

More than Triumphant! More than Victorious! More than "vanquish my enemies!" Overcoming them by force!

I am Strong, I am Wise, I am the Apple of my Father's eye. I can do all things through the strength He gives me. That's why each day I aspire to reach higher and higher, and I am thankful for the price Christ paid for my liberty.

Because of Him I am More, much, much more!

I am More than a Conqueror!

NOTES:

YOU KNOW YOU
(Know Yourself)

When disappointments come, don't just sit around
moping and whining! Celebrate yourself honey! With
special gifts and fine dinning!

And during those times it seems no one cares about you.
Care about yourself honey! Cheer yourself up! When
you feel blue!

REMEMBER! NOBODY KNOWS YOU BETTER
THAN YOU!

NOTES:

THOSE LOST DAYS
(Time Is Valuable)

Always so busy fighting for more! Never had time to
smell the roses! Working so hard to succeed in life!
Never noticed success was already in sight!

Those lost days, they never come back again! Not in the
way they were then! Since the day you were born! All of
those days are gone!

Neglecting Divine time given to dance! Thwarts yet
another steps ordered, perfect chance! Though, other
chances may come and go! If gone unnoticed, how will
you know?

Those lost days, they never come back again! Not in the
way they were then! Since the day you were born! All of
those days are gone!

NOTES:

DON'T DROP THE BALL
(Pass It On)

Life is filled with mysteries, just waiting to unfold.

Life is filled with histories, just waiting to be told.

When we listen at the distance and we hear that certain call. Please don't hesitate to answer, or once again you'll drop the ball.

NOTES:

CHAPTER FIVE

"TURN AROUND"

a moment

great house

i am that i am

w-i-s-d-o-m

meet me

guard your heart

turn around

the letter

more food for the soul

A MOMENT
(Essential)

Spirit of dreams coincides with reality dressed in amber
gold and white. Crowner of day and ruler of night!
Happy, bliss, dainty and free teaching all oh so silently.

Press forward my magnificent friend, indeed adieu.
We'll meet again! In my quiet atmosphere here, and in
the hereafter year after year.

Dorn yourself with brilliant light as we glide together
in mid flight, sparing no detail of our great triumph
knowing deservedly so we've never been stumped or
shaken in our endeavors forever more!

NOTES:

GREAT HOUSE
(To Walk Worthy)

Oh, I wanna be a, great house! Oh, I wanna be a, great
house! Oh, I wanna be a, great house!

A solid foundation sealed with love!

A great house is more than brick and mortar. A great
house has strength enough to stand. Filled with vessels
of precious gold and silver exuding brightness that
shines throughout the land.

Oh, I wanna be a, great house! Oh, I wanna be a, great
house! Oh, I wanna be a, great house!

A solid foundation sealed with love!

NOTES:

I AM THAT I AM
(Guess Who?)

Just as God said to Moses, when Moses asked, *"I AM THAT I AM!"* Readily I caught hold of the task. I started to think and I knew in a blink! I too am that I am!

I am that spirited baby which my mommy and daddy made, on a hot August day under the Magnolia shade!

"I am that I am"

I am that (scalp on fire) little girl running barefoot in the grass! Jumping fences made of bobbed wire, teaching Sunday school class and singing in the choir!

"I am that I am"

I am that young lady who grew ripe with age, and even when afraid, traveled to New York to perform on the stage!

"I am that I am"

I am that woman (though questionable it may seem), residing in Hollywood pursuing a dream. Working with children, my true hearts desire. Becoming a strong role model that they could admire. Gathering knowledge and wisdom to boot, sinking myself deeper in my spiritual root.

"I am that I am"

Yet, some still may wonder what type of character am
I? I love words! I love the arts! I love life! And banana
pie! To put it all in one book would require more than
a million pages! Cause I am all of my beginning, my
middle and my today! With all its' stages! Yes, I love to
sing! I love to act! And music makes me want to jam! In
quiet summation,
"I AM THAT I AM"!

W - I - S - D - O - M
(Stop Look Listen)

WISDOM! WISDOM!
The time is now for us to grow! And seek to know, the
truth that makes us free! To put works to faith and calm
the sea! Yes, receiving grace abundantly!

Wisdom is calling you! Wisdom is calling you! Make
the right choice! Listen to the voice! (of)

Wisdom calling you!

NOTES:

MEET ME
(In Our Secret Place)

Meet me in our secret place so I can walk with you, I wanna see your face. Meet me in our secret place so I can talk with you, and feel your warm embrace.

Meet me, meet me, meet me! Meet me in our secret place.

If ever I'm feeling alone and afraid, I think of when we are together. Remembering the time you saved me by grace giving me life eternal forever. Oh how I love you! Place no one above you! You're the one that I adore! Your goodness and mercy follows me evermore!

Meet me in our secret place so I can walk with you, I wanna see your face. Meet me in our secret place so I can talk with you and feel your warm embrace.

Meet me, meet me, meet me! Meet me in our secret place.

The love you give is more than enough to free those in bondage of the darkest power. I wanna tell them all of the safety found in your name so they too can take refuge in your strong tower.

Meet me in our secret place so I can walk with you, I wanna see your face. Meet me in our secret place so I can talk with you and feel your warm embrace.

Meet me, meet me, meet me! Meet me in our secret place.

NOTES:

GUARD YOUR HEART
(Self Love Secret)

When I was a little girl, my mommy and daddy said
to me:
*"Baby, this game of life is full of ups and downs. So,
a good strategy for you is to learn why you're around.
Keep a level head and a wise heart. And don't be afraid
to perform your part. Don't fall for fake knights on a
horse. Keep your focus, stay your course! Cause child,
all that glitters ain't gold! And those who bluff are not
so bold! The grass is not always greener on the other
side. And ya so called friends **will** take you for a ride.
So guard your heart, and keep your wits about yourself.
And never hide your Godly nature high on a shelf. Don't
drown your fears in that days' drug of choice. If you do,
you could lose your voice! (that can make a change in
this world). But, if you should slip and find yourself in a
trap of quick sand, be transformed! Renew your mind!
Then stand! Love yourself, and for your actions take full
responsibility. Continue seeking the truth, for the truth
you know shall make you free."* And they concluded
by saying: *"The secret of self love, is seeking wisdom
to help you grow, then rely on what you know. Don't do
everything that pleases you, because it seems permis-
sible to do so. Remember you can't truly love anybody
else, until you learn to love yourself. Cause ya see, that
drug called **Lust**, often masquerades as **Love**. Many a
soul, have lost their peace, placing their faith for protection in a rubber, (glove). But that's a bad habit you never
want to start. Therefore above all you do, be sure to*
Guard Your Heart!*"*

NOTES:

TURN AROUND
(Repent)

As I travel along this journey, life, I've experienced
some stormy weather. That has caused many of my
roads to become bunged and uncreative. Then being
forced to take a detour far off my path of purpose, I find
myself in unknown territory expected to behave like a
Native.

When suddenly I realize I've gone way beyond my exit,
and I fear that I just might lose my way. Then I see a
sign as plain as day! And ironically what does it say?
<u>"Turn Around!"</u> With an Arrow showing me the way.

But the voices from the strange land said, *"Hey, why
bother turning back toward that other place, maybe
this is where you're suppose to be. And who knows you
just might enjoy it here, why don't you stick around and
see."* Yet, I knew in my heart of hearts, the other place
was my Purpose and my Destiny. These merry making
Natives, all boisterous, jocund, larkish and gay, were
doing anything they pleased! Sporting vitiate displays!
And casting off all restraints feeling fanciful free!

I must admit it was all so tempting, and froth with
delight. Fulfilling the lust of the eyes, the lust of the
flesh, and the pride of life. Why not stay awhile! Why
not find a mate and cleave! It appeared to be so much
fun, it seemed only a fool would want to leave!

(I thought of joining them) But suddenly, I could not move a step and I didn't quite understand why. But my frozen feet gave me a chance to keenly spy, this strange land without its' fluff, and only then could I clearly see.
That, this place was filled with darkness and destruction! And I found ample reason to be alarmed! Because, everyone in this strange land was in bondage and no one was free. No one truly cared about anyone else, and each one would kill to save him self. It was hopeless, like they were all under a magic spell! Or some kind of deceptive agnostic charm!

A loud voice in my head screamed, *"What's your plan? You dope!"* Then a quiet voice from the depth of my soul arose within me saying, ***"Surely I know the plans I have for you, plans for your welfare and not for harm, to give you a future with hope!"***

Instantly, I was reminded of that "**Turn Around**" sign and Arrow I'd seen earlier showing me the way. It was lined with 66 books, filled with directions to obey! I remember that next to it stood a billboard, with words boldly printed inside **Bloody Hands**: ***"If my people who are called by my name humble themselves, pray, seek my face, and turn from their wicked ways, then will I hear from heaven. And will forgive their sin and heal their land"***

Right then I knew, exactly what I must do! I also learned, if ever again at a cross road I might be, when given the opportunity to "Turn Around!" I must hearken expeditiously!

THE LETTER

Dear Friend:

Did you know that we are inheritors of an enormous debt the moment we're born into this world? Curses upon curses handed down from generation to generation, over thousands and thousands of years? And no matter what **we** try to do, in our own power, to rid ourselves of that horrendous blight, stain and damnation, we find ourselves perishing in a state of darkness and deep depression. And slowly we keep slipping farther and farther away from our 'True Life Source'.

How unfair! What did we do to deserve such a fate?

Well, don't fret and don't be dismayed, I have "**Good News!**" For **you**! *"For God so loved the world that He gave His only begotten son that whosoever believeth on Him should not perish, but have everlasting life"*.

In that scriptural phrase we have been offered a wonderful gift. A gift of having our enormous debt **paid in full!** And all we have to do is receive that gift. You won't believe how simple it is. *"If we confess with our mouth that Jesus is Lord, and believe in our heart that God raised him from the dead we shall be saved"*. Yes! **Saved! Delivered! Freed!** You see, not only will this gift free us of that enormous debt, but we will also be raised and delivered out of darkness, out of that perishing state of depression, and translated into <u>Love's Pure Light.</u>

"For with the heart man believeth unto righteousness; and with the mouth confession is made unto salvation."

Wow! Believe it? Confess it? Receive it? Sounds too easy huh? Well, it's true. *"For everyone who calls on the Name of the LORD, **<u>with a sincere and repentant heart</u>**, shall be saved"!*

151

We should appreciate and honor this gift, for it is freely given to all. In the words of an old spiritual, *"Ain't that Good News!"* However, listen very carefully my friend, I can only make the introduction, it's up to **you** to develop the relationship!

Sincerely,

LOVE

MORE FOOD FOR THE SOUL

I believe that we all come into this life knowing everything we need to know. But then we go through some rough patches, like hardships, disappointments and pain, and we start to forget all the things that we know. Then after we've almost lived our entire lives being blinded by those rough patches, we finally come full circle back to what we already know.

If you don't get on that cycle, you'll stay true to what you know.

NOTES:

Forward ...

Yep, at the end!

There are about a million reasons that would validate the forward... at the end. But because I am not the author, I'll skip the first 1 thru 999,999. Instead, I'll fast forward to the one that is current, the one that matters most... ***Individuality! Yep. Individuality!!!!!!*** Total character, peculiar to and distinguishing one individual from others; distinct and of quality.

Ellia English and the word **"individuality"** are, (in my opinion) synonymous. It describes a journey well traveled. Not because of her endless love of children and all that concerns them... and not because of her **celebrity!** (That would be too easy.) Not that she finds more pleasure in prayer, than she does anything else in the course of her day. And I promise, it is not due to her honest nature or her obedient way. I can even confirm it is not her Godly quest for knowledge. In our 18+ year friendship, I can honestly say that her unique nature and unprecedented quality... or shall I say, her **"individuality"**, rest quietly on her **broad** shoulders, her **slim** hips, in her **full** lips and her **oriental** eyes. Her **wide** white feet secure her and her **strong** legs keep her fixed and firm. Her **"individuality"** rests someplace between her muscular build and her uncommonly dainty demeanor.

Every distinct external feature is a <u>unique </u>part of her internal makeup. Her **"individuality"** comes directly from **Spiritual molding and stretching**.... along with the part that only she could do... **plain old hard work!** Lovingly, the very same gift she is offering you.

Take it! Add to it the fruits of the Spirit, and a request for wisdom and viola! You have, (in my opinion,) what is so **perfectly <u>Ellia.</u>** The perfect gift from <u>her,</u> to **<u>you</u>**. Do something with it!

The forward at the end? Of course, (arrogantly), where else would it go?

ABOUT THE AUTHOR

Ellia English, born in Covington Georgia, developed an affinity for words in Kindergarten. Her teacher called her loquacious. Ellia loved the word loquacious. It was the most unique word she'd heard with the letter Q in it. (She had no idea it meant she talked too much).

Soon, Ellia developed a love for writing. And she honed her writing skills in high school penning award winning essays. One of which won her a Scholarship Fund from the Covington Kiwanis Club. In College Ellia studied music, speech and drama, however, after College Ellia continued her studies in writing by completing a Correspondence Course in Journalism and Short Story Writing.

While experiencing a successful career in the Entertainment Industry, Ellia continued to write in her spare time. She co wrote two Short Plays for a Theatrical Production "Please Sign In", that was well received by audiences in Los Angeles, which Ellia was also Director and Co Producer. Ellia is lovingly devoted to her passion and mission as mentor, aunt, and mother.

VERITY REFERENCES

NOTE: This novel is filled with writings from my **Personal Life Experiences.**
However, included within these pages are some of the writings I've reference from **the Word**"! **"The Word of God,"** never ceases to encourage me. May it encourage you as well!

BABY
Personal Life Experience
Proverb 22:6 *Train children in the right way, and when old, they will not stray.*

MY RAINBOW
Personal Life Experience
Genesis 9:11 15 *"And I will establish my covenant with you; neither shall all flesh be cut off any more by the waters of a flood to destroy the earth." And God said, "This is the token of the covenant which I make between me and you and every living creature that is with you, for perpetual generations; I do set my bow in the cloud and it shall be for a token of a covenant between me and the earth. And it shall come to pass, when I bring a cloud over the earth, that the bow shall be seen in the cloud; And I will remember my covenant, which is*

*between me and you and every living creature of all
flesh; and the waters shall no more become a flood to
destroy all flesh."*
Psalm 23:6a *Surely goodness and mercy shall follow me
all the days of my life.*
2ⁿᵈ Corinthians 5:18 *And all things are of God, who
hath reconciled us to himself by Jesus Christ, and hath
given to us the ministry of reconciliation.*
Colossians 1:27 *To whom God would make known
what is the riches of the glory of this mystery among the
Gentiles; which is Christ in you, the hope of glory.*

I'M YOUR CHILD
Personal Life Experience
Psalm 46:1 *God is our refuge and our strength, a very
present help in trouble.*

AFTER THE FALL
Personal Life Experience
Psalm 66:19 *But verily God hath heard me; he hath
attended to the voice of my prayer.*
Psalm 145:14, 18, 20a *The Lord upholdeth all that fall,
and raiseth up all those that he bowed down. The Lord
is nigh unto all those that call upon him, to all that call
upon him in truth. The Lord preserveth all those that
love him.*

THERE IS A LIGHT
Personal Life Experience
Psalm 119:105 *Thy word is a lamp unto my feet, and a
light unto my path*
Proverbs 4:7b *..... and with all thy getting get
understanding.*

GUARD YOUR HEART
Personal Life Experience
Romans 12:2 *And be not conformed to this world but be ye transformed by the renewing of your mind that ye may prove what is that good and acceptable, and perfect, will of God.*
John 8:32 *And ye shall know the truth and the truth shall make you free.*

WHAT TO DO (Question)
Personal Life Experience
Hebrews 11:6a *But without faith it is impossible to please him:*

WHAT TO DO (Answer)
Personal Life Experience
Hebrew 13:5b *...for he hath said, I WILL NEVER LEAVE THEE, NOR FORSAKE THEE.*
Psalm 121:3 4 *He will not suffer thy foot to be moved; he that keepeth thee will not slumber. Behold, he that keepeth Israel shall neither slumber nor sleep.*
Psalm 37:23 25 *The steps of a good man are ordered by the LORD: and he delighteth in his way. Though he fall, he shall not be utterly cast down; for the LORD upholdeth him with his hand. I have been young, and now am old; yet have I not seen the righteous forsaken, nor his seed begging bread.*
Matthew 7:7 8 *Ask, and it shall be given you; seek, and ye shall find; knock, and it shall be opened unto you: For every one that asketh receiveth; and he that seeketh findeth; and to himn that knocketh it shall be opened.*
John 4:24 *God is Spirit and they that worship him must worship him in spirit and in truth.*

2nd Timothy 2:15 *Study to shew thyself approved unto God, a workman that needeth not to be ashamed, rightly dividing the word of truth.*
Proverbs 4:23 *Keep thy heart with all diligence; for out of it are the issues of life.*
Proverbs 7:1 *My son, keep my words, and lay up my commands with thee.*
Proverbs 8:32b... *For blessed are they that keep my ways.*

GREAT HOUSE
Personal Life Experience
2nd Timothy **2:19 21** *Nevertheless, the foundation of God standeth sure, having this seal. The Lord knoweth them that are his. And, Let every one that nameth the name of Christ depart from iniquity. But in a great house there are not only vessels of gold and of silver, but also of wood and of earth; and some to honour, and some to dishonour. If a man therefore purge himself from these, he shall be a vessel unto honour, sanctified, and meet for the master's use and prepared unto every good work.*

CHOOSE YE THIS DAY
Personal Life Experience
John 3:16 *For God so loved the world that he gave his only begotten son that whosoever believeth in him should not perish, but have everlasting life*

WATER + BREAD + LIGHT + WORD
Personal Life Experience
John 6:35 & 41b *And Jesus said unto them, I am the bread of life: he that cometh to me shall never hunger; and he that believeth on me shall never thirst. ...I am the bread which came down from heaven.*

John 8:12b *I am the light of the world: he that followeth me shall not walk in darkness, but shall have the light of life.*

Jeremiah 2:13b ...*They have forsaken me the fountain of living waters, and hewed them out cisterns, broken cisterns, that can hold no water.*

John 6:63b ... *The words that I speak unto you, they are spirit, and they are life.*

John 1:5 & 9 10 *And the light shineth in darkness; and the darkness comprehended it not. .... That was the true light, which lighteth every man that cometh into the world. He was in the world, and the world was made by him, and the world knew him not.*

Lamentations 3:21 23 *That I recall to my mind, therefore have I hope. It is of the LORD'S mercies that we are not consumed, because his compassions fail not. They are new every morning; great is thy faithfulness.*

John 14:6 *Jesus saith unto him, I am the way, the truth, and the life, no man cometh unto the Father, but by me.*

Romans 8:34 *Who is he that condemeneth? It is Christ that died, yea rather, that is risen again, who is even at the right hand of God, who also maketh intercession for us.*

Hebrews 13:15 *By him therefore let us offer the sacrifice of praise to God continually, that is, the fruit of our lips giving thanks to his name.*

1ˢᵗ Corinthians 11:24 27 *And when he had given thanks, he brake it, and said, Take, eat; this is my body, which is broken for you: this do in remembrance of me. After the same manner also he took the cup, when he had supped, saying, This cup is the new testament in my blood; this do ye, as oft as ye drink it, in remembrance of me. For as often as ye eat this bread, and drink this cup, ye do shew the Lord's death till he come. Wherefore whosoever shall eat this bread, and drink this cup of the Lord, unworthily, shall be guilty of the body and blood of the Lord.*

1ˢᵗ Corinthians 15:54 55 *So when this corruptible shall have put on incorruption, and this mortal shall have put on immortality, then shall be brought to pass the saying that is written, Death is swallowed up in victory. O DEATH, WHERE IS THY STING? O GRAVE, WHERE IS THY VICTORY?* Hebrew 8:1 *Now of the things which we have spoken this is the sum; We have such an high priest, who is set on the right hand of the throne of the Majesty in the heavens.*

THE WORD IS A ROCK
Personal Life Experience

James 1:22 *But be ye doers of the word and not hearers only, deceiving your own selves.*

Matthew 7:24 27 *Therefore whosoever heareth these sayings of mine, and doeth them, I will liken him unto a wise man, which built his house upon a rock; And the rain descended, and the floods came, and the winds blew and beat upon that house; and it fell not; for it was founded upon a rock. And every one that hearteth these sayings of mine, and doeth them not, shall be likened unto a foolish man, which built his house upon the sand; And the rain descended, and the floods came, and the winds blew, and beat upon that house; and it fell and great was the fall of it.*

2ⁿᵈ Samuel 22:47 *The LORD liveth; and blessed be my rock; and exalted be the God of the rock of my salvation.*

Matthew 16:15 18 *He sayeth unto them, But whom say ye that I am? And Simon Peter answered and said, Thou art the Christ the Son of the living God. And Jesus answered and said unto him, Blessed art thou, Simon Barjona: for flesh and blood hath not revealed it unto thee, but my Father which is in heaven. And I say also unto thee, That thou art Peter; and upon this rock I will build my church; and the gates of hell shall not prevail against it.*

1st Corinthians 10:4 *And did all drink the same spiritual drink; for they drank of that spiritual Rock that followed them; and that Rock was Christ.*

1st Peter 2:5 9 *Ye also, as lively stones, are built up a spiritual house, an holy priesthood, to offer up spiritual sacrifices acceptable to God by Jesus Christ. Wherefore also it is contained in the scripture, BEHOLD, I LAY IN SION A CHIEF CORNER STONE, ELECT, PRECIOUS; AND HE THAT BELIEVETH ON HIM SHALL NOT BE CONFOUNDED. Unto you therefore which believe he is precious: but unto them which be disobedient, THE STONE WHICH THE BUILDERS DISALLOWED, THE SAME IS MAD THE HEAD OF THE CORNER. AND A STONE OF STUMBLING AND A ROCK OF OFFENCE, even to them which stumble at the word, being disobedient; whereunto also they were appointed. But ye are a chosen generation, a royal priesthood, an holy nation, a peculiar people; that ye should shew forth the praises of him who hath called you out of darkness into his marvelous light;*

Luke 20:17 *and he beheld them, and said What is this then that is written, THE STONE WHICH THE BUILDERS REJECTED, THE SAME IS BECOME THE HEAD OF THE CORNER?*

MORE:
Personal Life Experience
Proverbs 8:37 *Nay in all these things we are more than conquerors through him that loved us.*

LIVE STRONG AND PROSPER:
Personal Life Experience
3rd John 2 *Beloved, I wish above all things that thou mayest prosper and be in health, even as thy soul prospereth.*
Matthew 16:24 *Then said Jesus unto his disciples, if any man will come after me, let him deny himself, and take up his cross and follow me.* (see also **Mark 8:34 and Luke 9:23**)

GO:
Personal Life Experience
John 8:3 11 *And the scribes and Pharisees brought unto him a woman taken in adultery; and when they had set her in the midst, they say unto him, Master, this woman was taken in adultery, in the very act. Now Moses in the law commanded us, that such should be stoned; but what sayest thou? This they said, tempting him, that they might have to accuse him. But Jesus stooped down, and with his finger wrote on the ground, as tough he heard them not. So when they continued asking him, he lifted up himself and said unto them He that is without sin among you let him first cast a stone at her. And again he stooped down, and wrote on the ground. And they which heard it, being convicted by their own conscience, went out one by one, beginning at the eldest, even unto the last: and Jesus was left alone and the woman standing in the midst. When Jesus had lifted up himself, and saw none but the woman, he said unto her. Woman where are those thine accurers? Hath no man condemned thee? She said, No man, Lord. And Jesus said unto her, Neither do I condemn thee: go, and sin no more.*
1st John 1:9 *If we confess our sins, he is faithful and just to forgive us our sins, and cleanse us of all unrighteousness.*

MEET ME:
Personal Life Experience

Ephesian 2:8 *For by grace are ye saved through faith; and that not of yourselves; it is the gift of God.*

Romans 6:22 23 *But now being made free from sin, and become servants to God, ye have your fruit unto holiness, and the end everlasting life. For the wages of sin is death; but the gift of God is eternal life through Jesus Christ our Lord.*

Proverbs 18:10 *The name of the Lord is a strong tower; the righteous runneth into it and is safe.*

Psalm 23:6 *Surely goodness and mercy shall follow me all the days of my life:...*

Colossians 1:13 14 *Who hath delivered us from the power of darkness, and hath translated us into the kingdom of his dear Son. In whom we have redemption through his blood even the forgiveness of sins:*

WISDOM
Personal Life Experience

John 8:32 *And ye shall know the truth and the truth shall make you free.*

Romans 5:17 *For if by one man's offence death reigned by one; much more they which receive abundance of grace and of the gift of righteousness shall reign in life by one, Jesus Christ.*

James 2:20 *But wilt thou know, O vain man, that faith without works is dead?*

Proverbs 1:20 23 *Wisdom crieth without; she uttereth her voice in the streets: She crieth in the chief place of concourse, in the openings of the gates: in the city she uttereth her words, saying, How long, ye simple ones, will ye love simplicity? And the scorners delight in their scorning, and fools hate knowledge? Turn you at my*

167

reproof; behold, I will pour out my spirit unto you. I will make known my words unto you.

I AM THAT I AM
Personal Life Experience
Exodus 3:14 *And God said unto Moses, I AM THAT I AM; and he said Thus shalt thou say unto the children of Israel, I AM hath sent you.*

TURN AROUND
Personal Life Experience
Jeremiah 29:11 *For I know the thoughts I think toward you, saith the Lord, thoughts of peace, and not of evil, to give you an expected end.*
2 Chronicles 7:14 *If My people which are called by my name, shall humble themselves, and pray, and seek my face, and turn from their wicked ways; then will I hear from heaven, and forgive their sin, and heal their land.*
1st John 2:15 17 *Love not the world, neither the things that are in the world. If any man love the world, the love of the Father is not in him. For all that is in the world, the lust of the flesh, and the lust of the eyes, and the pride of life, is not of the Father, but is of the world. And the world passeth away, and the lust therof; but he that doeth the will of God abideth for ever.*

THE LETTER
Personal Life Experience
Romans 10:9 *That if thou shalt confess with thy mouth the Lord Jesus, and shalt believe in then heart that God hath raised him from the dead, thou shalt be saved.*
Romans 10:13 *For whosoever shall call upon the name of the Lord shall be saved.*
John 3:16 *For God so loved the world, that he gave his only begotten son, that whosoever believeth in him*

should not perish, but have everlasting life. Ephesian 2:8
For by grace are ye saved through faith; and that not of yourselves; it is the gift of God.
Romans 8:32 *He that spared not his own Son, but delivered him up for us all how shall he not with him also freely give us all things?*

NOTES:

CPSIA information can be obtained at www.ICGtesting.com
Printed in the USA
LVOW060857061111

253720LV00003B/69/P